ELMER TAKES OFF

David McKee

HarperCollins*Publishers*

It was a very, very windy day. Elmer, the patchwork elephant, was sheltering in a cave with his elephant friends, some birds, and Cousin Wilbur, who was playing tricks with his voice. The elephants laughed when Wilbur made his voice come from a hole at the back of the cave.

All morning long the wind howled.

"It's not a good day for flying," said a bird.

"It's a good day to be a heavy elephant," said Elmer. "An elephant can't be blown away."

"I bet even *you* are afraid to go out in *this* wind, Elmer," said the bird.

"Afraid?" said Elmer. "Not me! Come on, Wilbur."

"Come back! Don't be silly!" called the elephants.

But Elmer and Wilbur had already gone out into the wind.

When they were behind some trees and out of sight,
Elmer led the way into another cave.
   "You're up to something, Elmer," said Wilbur.
   Elmer laughed. "Let's play a trick," he said.
"Make your voice come from outside, as if we were

still walking away. Sound like me sometimes."

"I get it," said Wilbur. He made his voice come from the distance. "It's hard to move in this wind," he said, sounding like Elmer. Then, sounding like himself, he called, "Careful, Elmer! Hold on!"

The elephants heard the voices and began to worry.
"Hold on to something, Elmer!" Wilbur called.
"Look out!"

"HELP!" came Elmer's voice. "HELP! I'm flying!"
"ELMER, COME BACK!" came Wilbur's voice. "OH, HELP! HELP!"

"Elmer's being blown away," said an elephant.
"We must help."

"If you go out, you'll be blown away too," said
the bird.

"Form a chain," said another elephant, "trunks
holding tails."

The elephants crept out of the cave, each holding
on to the tail of the elephant in front.

"Look at them," said Elmer, laughing. "They look so funny."

"Go back," teased Wilbur. "You'll be blown away!"

The elephants all began to speak at once. "We've been fooled!" "It's an Elmer and Wilbur trick!" Then they backed into their cave, looking funnier than ever.

When Elmer and Wilbur and all the elephants were safely back
in the cave, everyone enjoyed the joke.

"That was very funny, Elmer," said the bird. "But you really
could have been blown away, you know."

"Really, Bird," said Elmer, "an elephant can't blow away. I'll
walk to those trees and back to prove it."

"He's up to another trick," said an elephant as Elmer walked
away.

They all watched as Elmer disappeared behind some trees.

Then they heard Elmer's voice calling, "Help! I can't keep my feet on the ground!"

The elephants laughed. "Very funny, Wilbur," they said.

"HELP!" the voice called again. "I'M FLYING!"

The elephants laughed louder than ever.

"It's not me this time," said Wilbur.

"Look!" said the bird. "It *isn't* Wilbur!"
The elephants stared. There was Elmer, high above the trees.
"What's he doing up there?" gasped an elephant.
"It's called flying," said the bird.
"Poor Elmer," said an elephant.

It's my ears, thought Elmer. They're acting like wings. How will I ever get down?

Wilbur and the others looked very small as Elmer flew off into the distance.

But after a while, Elmer began to enjoy himself. He looked down at all the other animals sheltering from the wind. They were all staring up at him, surprised to see an elephant fly by.

"It's Elmer," said a lion, "up to another of his tricks."

At last the wind died down and Elmer landed.
Oh, dear, he thought. It's going to be a long walk
home. It serves me right for being so silly.
And he set off to find home.

Meanwhile, the birds and the elephants had set off to find Elmer.

"He's over here!" called the birds, and everyone rushed to meet Elmer and hear about his adventure.

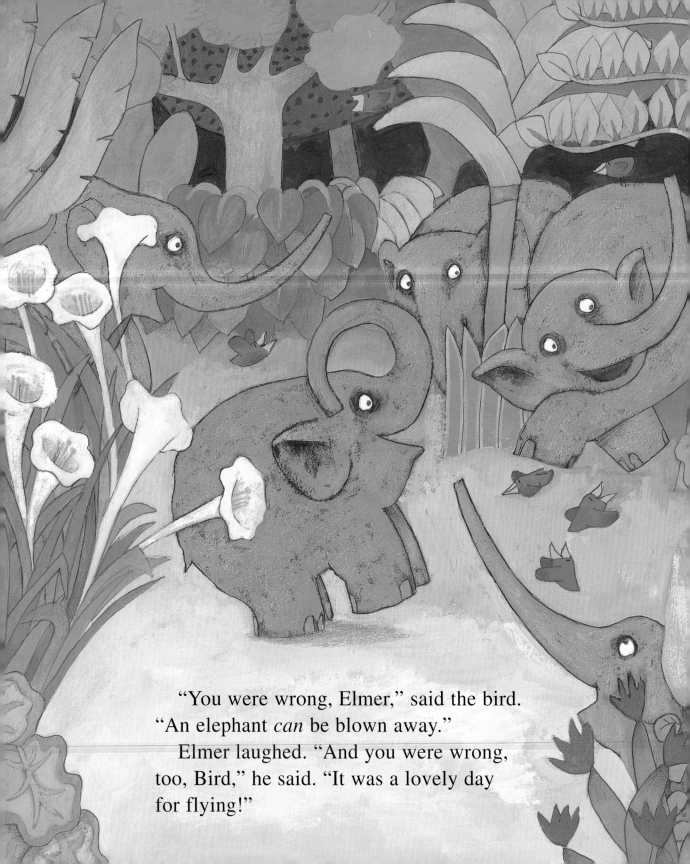

"You were wrong, Elmer," said the bird.
"An elephant *can* be blown away."
   Elmer laughed. "And you were wrong,
too, Bird," he said. "It was a lovely day
for flying!"

In memory of Barbara
with love and thanks
for Chantel, Chuck, and Brett

First published in Great Britain by Andersen Press Ltd.

Library of Congress Cataloging-in-Publication Data
McKee, David.
Elmer takes off / David McKee.
p. cm.
Summary: On a very, very windy day Elmer, the patchwork elephant, assures all the other
animals and birds that nothing could ever blow him away.
[1. Elephants—Fiction. 2. Flight—Fiction. 3. Wind—Fiction.] I. Title.
PZ7.M19448Eme 1998 [E]—dc21 97-19121 CIP AC

U.S. Edition 1 2 3 4 5 6 7 8 9 10

Printed in Italy

First paper-over-board edition, 2004